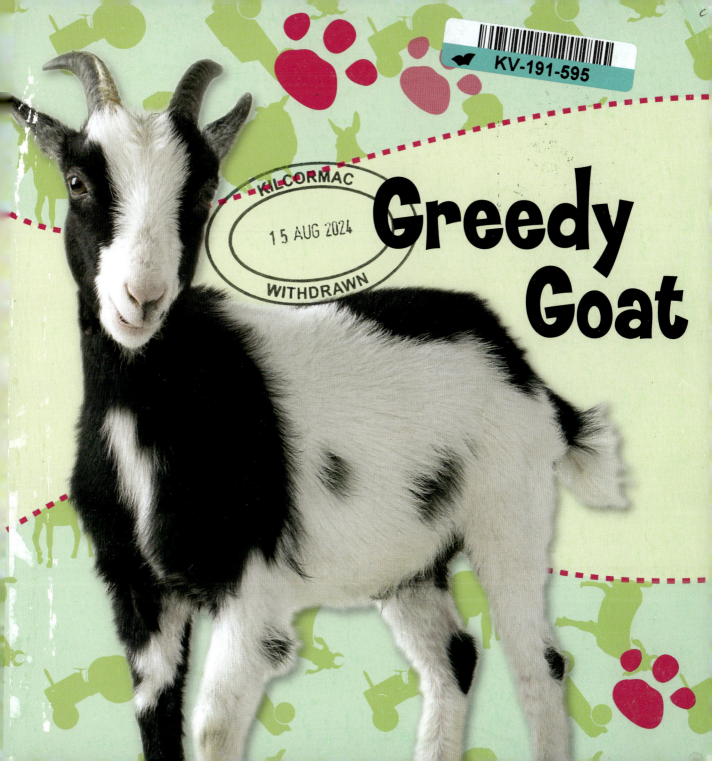

Greedy Goat

It's a beautiful day on Big Barn Farm
and Gobo is really hungry. He's always hungry!
He seems to have completely forgotten he's
only just eaten his lunch!

"Do you have any food, Digger?" asks Gobo.
"I have some dog biscuits left," Digger replies.
Gobo quickly eats all of Digger's biscuits.
Oh dear! Poor Digger.

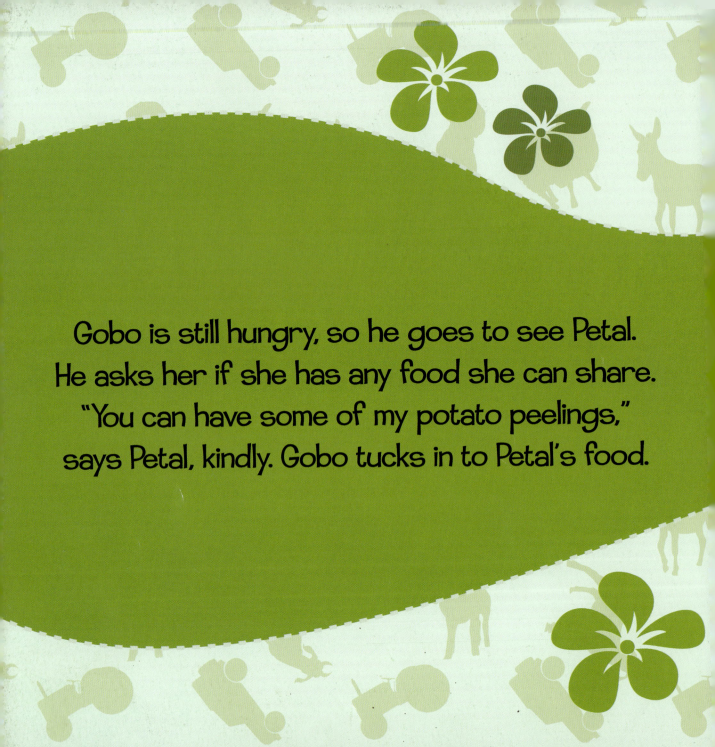

Gobo is still hungry, so he goes to see Petal.
He asks her if she has any food she can share.
"You can have some of my potato peelings,"
says Petal, kindly. Gobo tucks in to Petal's food.

Soon after, Gobo finds Dash and even though he doesn't like it, he gulps down his food too! But Gobo's still very hungry. Where could he go next?

The farmhouse - that's it! Gobo races to the farmhouse and finds an apple pie sitting on the window ledge. He peers in and starts to eat it. "Gobo! That's my pie!" cries the farmer's wife.

Gobo runs from the farmhouse as quickly as he can and finds Lester's coop. He's just about to ask Lester for some food, when he sees something in the distance - a picnic!

The picnic is in the field beyond the barn. "I'm sure those people wouldn't mind me eating their food," thinks Gobo. "I'll walk there slowly and make sure nobody sees me, just in case."

Soon after, Gobo creeps over to the picnic food, very slowly and very carefully. "There's a lot of food, but which would make the best snack for me?" wonders Gobo.

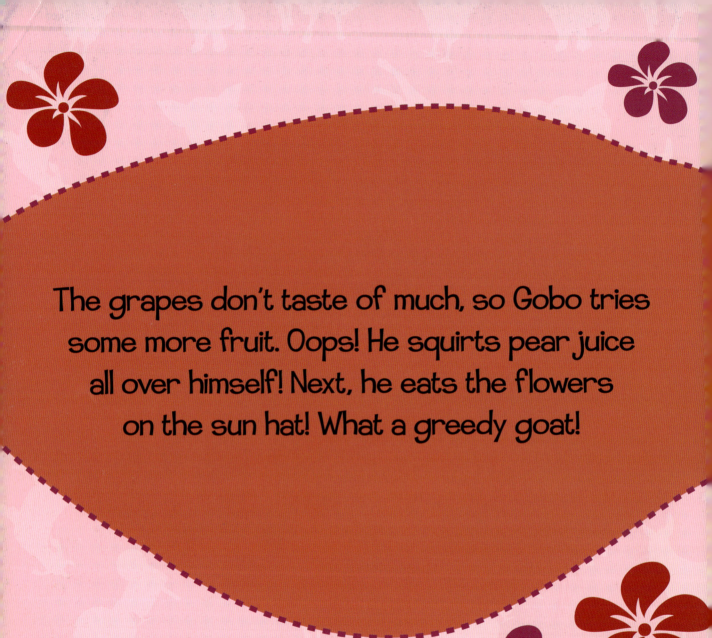

The grapes don't taste of much, so Gobo tries some more fruit. Oops! He squirts pear juice all over himself! Next, he eats the flowers on the sun hat! What a greedy goat!

The Farmyard Bunch come over to see Gobo. "Guess what?" gasps Petal. "The farmer's just called us. It's feeding time again." "Argh!" groans Gobo, very loudly!

Oh dear! With all the dog biscuits, potato peelings, hay, grapes, pears and flowers, Gobo has eaten so much food, he is finally full up and won't be able to eat his dinner!